Healthy Heath

and His Magic Fruits and Vegetables

A Book about Kids' Nutrition, Kindness, and
Celebrating Individuality

By Dr. Kristen Poe

This book is dedicated to my loving family and friends, but especially FDP, GG, VIP, and MVP.

You are truly my inspiration, the loves of my life, and my "why" in everything I do. You are my greatest blessings and I love you.

This is the story of Healthy Heath and his magic fruits and vegetables. Although he looked ordinary, Heath was actually a very extraordinary boy.

Some of his favorite things to do were gymnastics and yoga with his mom and dad and three sisters, reading books, and learning new things at school.

His classmates were all amazed at how smart he was. In fact, he was the smartest kid in school! He loved going to school!

However, most of all he loved eating vegetables and fruits. Every chance Heath had, he would eat yummy fruits and vegetables. In fact, when he ate all of his fruits and vegetables, especially green vegetables, he got super special powers.

He especially loved to eat spinach, broccoli, carrots, and blueberries. When he ate his fruits and vegetables, he could grow big muscles and turn into a superhero with his magical powers.

He could jump so high that he could reach the top of a tree. He could lift a car or a huge rock over his head. He could run like lighting, and he could solve math problems and read books in less than one minute. He got straight A's in school.

Only Heath's parents knew about his special superhero powers. They made sure to let him know how special and wonderful he was each day. But none of his classmates at school knew about his special powers.

In fact, Heath was a small boy! However, he knew as soon as he ate his fruits and vegetables, he would turn into a brainiac superhero.

Every day, during snack time at school, Heath would have a big bowl of green vegetables and berries. He loved snack time because it gave him a lot of energy. It helped him learn and get good grades. His fruits and vegetables also gave him his secret special powers and kept him healthy.

However, Healthy Heath had a classmate named Billy the Bully who would tease him every day about his healthy snacks and lunches.

Billy the Bully was a lot bigger than Heath and would say, "Heath, you always eat vegetables and fruits and all this strange stuff that looks so boring and gross. YUCK! Why don't you eat something fun like all of us? I have my cookies and chips for a snack. I don't see anyone else in this class eating like you! No one wants to play with you or eat snacks with you because you are so different!"

Many of the other kids would laugh with Billy. Healthy Heath would feel sad, but he was always kind and helpful to all of his classmates. He didn't let the teasing stop him from eating his healthy foods, always being kind, and having his superpowers.

Heath did enjoy eating cake and sweet treats on his birthday and other special occasions, but he really enjoyed eating his fruits and vegetables. He called them his "superhero foods."

However, Heath did have one special friend named Sensitive Sienna. Sienna would quietly watch Billy the Bully be unkind and tease Healthy Heath because he was different.

She would say to Billy, "You are not being very nice to Heath. You eat a lot of sugar and junk food. You should try sharing his healthy snacks sometime and stop teasing him!" She would say to Heath, "Don't listen to Billy. He is mean. I think it is great that you eat all of these fruits and vegetables. I love them too! Can I have some with you?"

Every day, Heath would share his fruits and vegetables with Sensitive Sienna, and they would eat together and talk. Heath was happy to have a great friend like Sienna.

During snack time one day, Healthy Heath found out from his teacher, Mrs. Motivator, that they were going to have two very special guests visit his classroom.

It was going to be two of his heroes, Olympic athletes Will the Weight Lifter and Gina the Gymnast. His entire classroom cheered when they found out they would get to meet them!

The night before Will the Weight Lifter and Gina the Gymnast visited Heath's classroom, he was so excited he could barely sleep. He woke up the next morning and ran downstairs.

"Mom and Dad, I am so excited to meet my heroes Will and Gina today. They are so strong and healthy and happy. I really hope I can take a picture with them so I never forget this day. It would make me so happy! This is going to be the best day ever!"

When he got to school, all of his classmates were so excited. They were all laughing and giggling and waiting patiently for Will the Weight Lifter and Gina the Gymnast to arrive. As usual, the students had their morning snacks before their special guests arrived.

Today Heath had carrots and blueberries for a snack. As usual, Billy the Bully came up to him and teased him. "Heath, you really eat strange food, yuck! You eat so many fruits and vegetables. My snacks are so much better than yours."

Heath did not pay any attention to Billy the Bully today. He was too excited about Will the Weight Lifter and Gina the Gymnast coming to his classroom.

As usual, Sensitive Sienna came over to Healthy Heath and asked to share his yummy healthy snacks.

After snack time, Mrs. Motivator called all of the students to sit in a circle. All of the children clapped and cheered when Will the Weight Lifter and Gina the Gymnast arrived. They talked about how hard they practiced every day to become Olympic athletes.

"Practice makes perfect. You have to work hard and focus, and you will achieve all of your goals and dreams. It is so important to read books, study and learn, exercise, get a good night's sleep, be kind to everyone, and eat healthy foods."

Billy the Bully raised his hand and said, "Will, you are my hero. I want to be an Olympic weight lifter, and be big and strong like you someday!"

"Well, besides eating healthy, a big part of being successful is being kind to others."

Billy the Bully looked down at his feet because he knew he was not always nice to Healthy Heath.

Billy the Bully stood up and looked over at Healthy Heath and said to Will and Gina, "I want to say sorry to Heath. I have not always been nice to him because he is different and eats all of these weird foods like fruits and vegetables all of the time."

Billy the Bully looked at Healthy Heath and said, "I am sorry, Heath, I will never tease you or anyone else again."

Heath smiled and said, "That's okay, Billy. I accept your apology!"

Gina said, "Now that is the start of a friendship and being a hero!"

"One of the things that makes each and every one of us wonderful is that we are all different! We all have different talents and ideas that make us special. We should always accept and celebrate what makes us all different. As for eating healthy, Heath eats many of the great foods that we eat as Olympic athletes."

"He does?" said Billy the Bully.

"Yes," said Will. "I was watching him during snack time today, and he had carrots and blueberries, which are so healthy. It is so important to eat as many vegetables as we can every day. They give us special vitamins that our body needs to grow big and strong and stay healthy. Fruits like blueberries have special things in them called antioxidants and phytonutrients. They give our fruits and vegetables their beautiful bright colors and keep us healthy. I can tell you that all athletes and superheroes make sure they eat their fruits and vegetables every day."

"WOW!" said Billy the Bully. "I am going to start eating my fruits and vegetables every day, too, like Heath! What else should we eat?"

"Well, you also want to make sure you are eating healthy protein every day. Protein helps us to build our muscles and stay big and strong. Some great things to eat to get protein are eggs, chicken, turkey, fish, beans, tofu, nuts, and seeds. We also get protein from dairy like milk, cheese, and yogurt."

"I eat all of those things!" Heath exclaimed.

"We also want to make sure we are eating healthy carbohydrates!"

"Carbo-what?" asked Sensitive Sienna.

"Carbohydrates! They provide our body with energy, and they are the fuel for our bodies."

"Is it like when we stop at the gas station with our parents to fill our car up with gas?" asked Heath.

"YES!" exclaimed Gymnast Gina. "That's a great example, Heath. Carbohydrates give our body the fuel we need to go, like filling a car up with gas so it can drive!"

Billy the Bully asked, "So what kinds of foods are carbohydrates?"

Will the Weight Lifter said, "There are many things, but some good things we can have are whole-wheat bread and pasta, beans, oatmeal, rice, potatoes, and whole-wheat crackers."

"Yes, I eat all of those too!" exclaimed Healthy Heath.

"There is one last thing we want to make sure we are eating every day too. It is what we call fats."

"Fats are good for us?" asked Sensitive Sienna. "I thought I heard my mommy and daddy say they were not good one time."

Gina the Gymnast said, "There are certain kinds of fats that are not good for us, like fried foods such as french fries and fried chicken. But healthy fats are like little building blocks that can help give us the energy to run and play and learn in school. They help us stay warm so we are not cold all of the time, and they help protect our hearts. Some great things we can eat to get good fats are avocados, coconuts, butter, peanut butter, almond butter, sunflower butter, and salmon."

Health Heath stood up and exclaimed, "I eat all of those too!"

Billy the Bully asked, "What about yummy stuff like cake, ice cream, and cookies?"

"Yes," said Gina, "these things taste yummy. You can enjoy these things once in a while. It is a lot of fun to share a sweet snack with friends every now and then. But these things all have added sugar, which is not very good for our health. It is not good for our teeth and can make us tired and sluggish if we eat too much."

Billy asked, "So it's okay to have an ice cream sundae or cookies with my parents and sister on the weekend, but not every day, right?"

"Exactly, Billy," said Gina.

Heath couldn't contain his excitement anymore. He ran over to his lunch box and pulled out his lunch to show Will the Weight Lifter and Gina the Gymnast. He had chicken, a slice of whole-wheat bread, sunflower butter, broccoli, apples, yogurt, and water for lunch.

"I think I have my protein and dairy, carbohydrates, fats, and fruits and vegetables all here!" he said.

"You sure do!" Will the Weight Lifter exclaimed. "Heath's lunch looks exactly like the meals Gymnast Gina and I eat every day to stay healthy and strong and have a lot of energy!"

Healthy Heath was so excited, he jumped up and down and forgot about his superpowers. He jumped so high that the top of his head touched the ceiling, and he lifted the entire bookshelf over his head out of excitement. He suddenly had large muscles and was wearing a cape! All of his classmates shouted with excitement and couldn't believe it.

"Heath is a superhero! He is strong because of his healthy foods and fruits and vegetables. Yay for Heath!"

Will the Weightlifter and Gina the Gymnast could not believe how strong he was.

"Yes, he has special powers and eats very healthy. He is a great example for all of us! Although we may not all have superpowers like Heath, eating lots of fruits and vegetables will keep us healthy. They will give us the energy we need to achieve everything we want to."

Will the Weight Lifter said, "Heath, thank you for setting a wonderful example for all of your classmates and always being kind to everyone. Would you like to take a picture with Gina the Gymnast and me?"

Heath exclaimed, "Yes, I am so excited. You and Gina are my heroes! This has been the best day ever!"

After Heath took a photograph with Will the Weight Lifter and Gina the Gymnast, they invited the entire class to take a picture together.

"Let's not forget this great day together. Always be kind and loving to each other, celebrate all of our wonderful differences, eat less junk food, and don't forget to eat your fruits and vegetables!"

Made in the USA
Las Vegas, NV
19 April 2021